love your library

Buckinghamshire Libraries

Search, renew or reserve online 24/7
www.buckscc.gov.uk/libraries

24 hour renewal line
0303 123 0035

Enquiries
01296 382415

follow us **twitter**

@Bucks_Libraries

For Mia
R.I.

For Finley and Fred
K.M.

ORCHARD BOOKS

First published in Great Britain in 2016 by The Watts Publishing Group

1 3 5 7 9 10 8 6 4 2

Text © Rose Impey 2016

Illustrations © Katharine McEwen 2016

A CIP catalogue record for this book is available from the British Library.

ISBN 978 1 40832 525 4 (HB)
ISBN 978 1 40832 531 5 (PB)

Printed in China

The paper and board used in this book are made from wood from responsible sources

Orchard Books
An imprint of Hachette Children's Group
Part of The Watts Publishing Group Limited
Carmelite House, 50 Victoria Embankment, London EC4Y 0DZ

An Hachette UK Company
www.hachette.co.uk
www.hachettechildrens.co.uk

SIR LANCE-A-LITTLE

and the VERY WICKED WITCH

Rose Impey · Katharine McEwen

ORCHARD

Cast of Characters

Sir Lance-a-Little

Harold the Horse

Princess Plum

Huffalot the Dragon

The Very Wicked Witch

The few times Sir Lance-a-Little
had actually fought the dragon,
neither had won. It was always
a draw.

Sir Lance-a-Little needed a new tactic, a way to defeat Huffalot, once and for all. And he knew just where to find it.

HUNDRED FAMOUS FIGHTS

KNOW YOUR FOE

FIGHTING TALK

DRAGON FIGHTS

But it was hard to concentrate with his pestiferous cousin, Princess Plum, pestering him as usual.

"Go away!" Sir Lance-a-Little told her in the end.

Finally, Sir Lance-a-Little found his new idea: The Element of Surprise! He'd never tried that! Usually, he sent a challenge warning Huffalot he was coming. Today he would surprise him!

Aha!

DRAGON FIGHTING TIPS AND TRICKS by ARTHUR KING →

Outside the castle, Princess Plum had an idea of her own. She would go on ahead of her cousin to Huffalot's cave. She would be there, waiting, when he arrived.

Sir Lance-a-Little rode along on his trusty horse, Harold, armed with his pointy lance … and his sharp sword … and his shiny shield.

He pictured Huffalot snoring in his cave, completely unaware that his No. 1 enemy was on his way. Today was the day that Huffalot would huff his last!

By and by, Sir Lance-a-Little came
to a clearing, where a Very Wicked
Witch was stirring a cauldron.
Nearby, on a rock, sat a rather
familiar-looking frog!

You wait
till my cousin
gets you!

It sounded familiar, too.

Sir Lance-a-Little was tempted to ride on, but he knew the Knights' Code of Honour. And rescuing princesses, even annoying ones like his cousin, was top of the list.

But today Sir Lance-a-Little didn't march straight up to the witch and demand she take the spell off his cousin. This time, he would try his new tactic: The Element of Surprise!

Aha!

He hid behind a bush and waited
to see what the witch was up to.
She was clearly making a spell.

One by one, she dropped things into her cauldron as she chanted out loud:

"Snake's rattle … Bee's sting,

Rat's tail … Bat's wing,

Cat's fur … Rabbit's paw,

Frog's legs … Hmmm."

The witch was about to throw
the frog into the cauldron,
legs and all.

But she stopped and muttered,
"Oh, darn and dust it. Forgot the
dragon's claw!"

Aha! thought Sir Lance-a-Little, bobbing up from his hiding place. "I think I could help you there," he told the Very Wicked Witch, who was rather surprised.

She was even more surprised
when he offered to take her to
Huffalot's cave and give her *all* the
dragon's claws.

"After I defeat him, of course," he
added.

The witch rubbed her bony hands
in glee.

"But first," said Sir Lance-a-Little, "you must turn this frog back into my annoying little cousin."

The witch was very wicked, but she was also very cunning. It was no easy matter to find a dragon, whereas she could easily find another frog, or another princess she could turn into one!

She muttered a few magic words,
and suddenly there was Princess
Plum, sitting on the rock looking
hot and cross.

"Now, let's get going!" screeched the witch.

As they rode along, the Very Wicked Witch flew over their heads on her broomstick.

"Get a move on," she kept telling them, but Harold refused to be hurried.

Hurry up!

Princess Plum asked Sir Lance-a-
Little how he meant to defeat the
dragon this time.

"Aha!" he said, proudly.

"The Element of Surprise! This
time Huffalot doesn't know
I'm coming."

Uh-oh! thought Princess Plum. She decided not to tell her cousin that she had visited the dragon earlier and told Huffalot that his No. 1 enemy was on his way.

So when they reached Huffalot's cave, the dragon had already filed his teeth … sharpened his claws … and fed his fire. He was more than ready for a fight.

RRRAGHHHH!

The witch kept well away from the dragon. "Go and get me those claws," she hissed at Sir Lance-a-Little, "like you promised."

When Huffalot heard this, he was furious. No way was that pointy-nosed witch getting hold of his claws! The dragon opened his mouth and huffed …

and puffed …

Huge flames licked up into
the sky, setting light to the
witch's broomstick.

"He-l-l-lp!" she shrieked as she
disappeared into the distance.

Sir Lance-a-Little and the dragon watched her go.

"And how exactly did you plan to defeat me this time?" Huffalot asked Sir Lance-a-Little.

The little knight smiled as he remembered his new tactic. "Aha!" was all he said. He would save that for another day, when it would come as a complete surprise.

SIR LANCE-A-LITTLE

Join the bravest knight in Notalot
for all his adventures!

Written by Rose Impey • Illustrated by Katharine McEwen

❏ Sir Lance-a-Little and the
Big Bad Wolf

978 1 40832 520 9 (HB)
978 1 40832 526 1 (PB)

❏ Sir Lance-a-Little and the
Three Angry Bears

978 1 40832 521 6 (HB)
978 1 40832 527 8 (PB)

❏ Sir Lance-a-Little and the
Most Annoying Fairy

978 1 40832 522 3 (HB)
978 1 40832 528 5 (PB)

❏ Sir Lance-a-Little and the
Terribly Ugly Troll

978 1 40832 523 0 (HB)
978 1 40832 529 2 (PB)

❏ Sir Lance-a-Little and the
Ginormous Giant

978 1 40832 524 7 (HB)
978 1 40832 530 8 (PB)

❏ Sir Lance-a-Little and the
Very Wicked Witch

978 1 40832 525 4 (HB)
978 1 40832 531 5 (PB)

Orchard Books are available from all good bookshops, or can be ordered from our website:
www.orchardbooks.co.uk
or telephone 01235 400400, or fax 01235 400454.

Prices and availability are subject to change.